LuLu and Boo Meet Banjo

Roxanne Rudkin

Acknowledgement:

I would like to thank my family and friends for their love and encouragement. LuLu and Boo will have many adventures because of them. A special thanks to Don whose precise and maddening attention to detail makes everything work.

LuLu and Boo Meet Banjo
Copyright 2019 by Roxanne Rudkin

Tellwell Talent
www.tellwell.ca

ISBN
978-0-2288-0234-1 (Hardcover)
978-0-2288-0233-4 (Paperback)

For "Big Eyes"
and a little boy named
Elliott

LuLu and Boo are two very happy housecats. They have a wonderful life with their owners, Missy Quinn and Mister Sam. They love to sleep all day in their warm and cozy sunroom and play all night after Sam and Quinn come home from work. They chase all their fun toys about the house and take plenty of breaks for pets and scratches.

Because they are house cats they almost never go outside. Missy Quinn and Mister Sam have always cautioned them of the hidden dangers of the world outside. There was never any need to step their furry feet outdoors and no reason to get them dirty. Boo was especially fussy and liked his feet clean at all times.

One Friday afternoon LuLu was waking up from a long nap with delicious salmon loaf on her mind. Normally the food dish was full of crunchy nuggets, but Fridays were different. It was soft food night and LuLu's favourite was salmon. She couldn't wait for Missy Quinn and Mister Sam to come home. Boo was already awake and cleaning his feet.

When they heard a familiar noise outside, LuLu and Boo scampered over to the front door to meet their owners as they walked in. This was the best part of the day for LuLu and Boo. There was always so much snuggling and cuddling.

LuLu trotted over to the food dish meowing politely to remind everyone it was time for dinner. But something was different. No one followed. Missy Quinn and Mister Sam were talking quietly to themselves and giggling.

"What are they saying, Boo? Can you hear?" LuLu asked.

"Something about a walk," said Boo. "Outside?" he added, sounding puzzled.
"This can't be about us! What about the salmon loaf?" LuLu asked wondering if they had forgotten.

What came next was completely unusual and quite a surprise. Sam picked up Boo and announced they were all going for a walk before dinner. LuLu looked at Boo, his eyes round and confused, as he dangled from Sam's arms. They were both very puzzled. Sam and Quinn didn't like them going outside. Only once, a long time ago, they had left the sunroom on an outdoor adventure. Missy Quinn and Mister Sam had been very worried and afraid for their safety.

Now, for no apparent reason, Mister Sam and Missy Quinn were breaking the rules. They carried LuLu and Boo outside and placed them on the grass.

"Ah! This feels nice," thought Boo as his feet touched the nice soft grass. "This will be fun," he said to LuLu as she crouched low to the ground.

Boo's excitement quickly disappeared as Sam and Quinn put circle-like harnesses around their bodies. They were attached to long ropes. Sam called it a leash. They had never heard that word before.

"What is this?" said Boo. "I hate this rope!"

"I feel silly tied to this thing," LuLu replied.

None of this felt good. LuLu and Boo did not like the feel of the harness around their tummies. They were encouraged to take a few steps as Sam and Quinn gently tugged on the leashes, but LuLu was stubborn and stood firm. This was not fun at all. LuLu felt miserable. She just wanted to go back in the house and have dinner. Boo flopped to the grass and lay on his side refusing to move.

Suddenly something caught LuLu's attention. In the distance stood a small hedge, with eyes! Something was watching them. LuLu looked more closely, and she was sure she saw bright white teeth in a smile.

"Boo! Look at that bush over there!" LuLu meowed loudly.

Boo turned toward the bush, and he too could see the creature.

"I think it's laughing!" Boo said.

"Oh no, this is awful," said LuLu.

Not only were they miserable attached to their leashes, but now someone was watching and thought it was funny.

Finally, realizing no one was going for a walk, Sam and Quinn picked up the cats and went back inside the house.

"Thank goodness. That was awful," said LuLu as she was carried back through the doorway. "Maybe now we can eat."

Boo immediately sat down to start cleaning his feet. "Who do you think was looking at us from the bush?" asked Boo.

"I don't know, but I do know that I'm hungry!" said LuLu as she purred when Missy Quinn served her the salmon loaf.

The next day, LuLu and Boo were curled up in their beds just about to fall asleep for their afternoon nap. They could hear Sam and Quinn leaving the house but knew they would return home shortly as they were never gone very long on a Saturday. A few minutes later, LuLu thought she heard the sound of feet softly walking about the house. She slowly opened one eye to make sure Boo was still snuggled in his bed and slowly closed it again. "I must have been dreaming," she thought.

Suddenly, there was a loud voice in the sunroom.

"Hey there, cool cats!"

LuLu and Boo both jumped off their beds, terrified!

"WHO ARE YOU?" LuLu exclaimed. "HOW DID YOU GET IN HERE?"

Standing in the hallway was the strangest looking cat. It was scruffy and dirty, and its hair stood out all over the place.

"Well, someone needs a good grooming," Boo said to himself as he stared at the stranger. "Oh my, and what's that smell?" he thought as his nose crinkled up from the unpleasant odour.

"The door was left open a crack, and I snuck in before your people closed it. Banjo's my name. I live outside. I'm an alley cat. Nice house you have here."

Banjo turned and walked away. LuLu and Boo peered around the corner as Banjo leaped on the sofa and rolled around on his back atop the comfy cushions.

"Ah, this is lovely," Banjo said and then he suddenly jumped off the sofa, ran across the rug and onto the chair. Little puffs of dust followed behind. He was smiling, and all his teeth were showing. LuLu and Boo knew right away this was the creature that had been watching them from the bushes the day before.

Banjo jumped up again and ran down the hallway.

"Hey! Stop!" Boo yelled and chased after him.

"What is happening?" LuLu thought as she watched in horror. "This is terrible. Missy Quinn and Mister Sam will be home soon, and what will they think when they see this crazy cat tearing around?"

Banjo laughed as he ran and jumped on everything with Boo chasing after him. Across the bed and back down the hallway, Banjo knocked over a plant as he tried to jump over it. LuLu stood wide eyed and frozen. She didn't know what to do.

Suddenly, the chaos ended as Boo stopped outside the bathroom door. LuLu ran toward him and could see the bewildered look on his face. She looked inside the bathroom and could not believe her eyes. This cat was drinking water right out of the toilet!

"WHAT ARE YOU DOING? THAT"S DISGUSTING!" shouted LuLu. "There's water in the dish by our food!"

"What?" asked Banjo with a big smile on his face. "It's clean water; I'm used to drinking out of puddles."

Without warning, the front door opened. All three cats froze, their ears pointed up to hear. LuLu was afraid that Missy Quinn and Mister Sam would be angry with the mess this strange uninvited visitor had made. As Sam and Quinn came into the house, LuLu and Boo could hear another voice. Their friend Lauren was with them. LuLu and Boo loved Lauren. She was so nice and always had treats for them.

The three cats walked slowly to the door. Missy Quinn, Mister Sam, and Lauren stopped talking and looked over at them. LuLu closed her eyes expecting something bad to happen, but to her surprise, they all started laughing!

"Who is this?" Lauren said as she picked up Banjo. Sam and Quinn smiled and pet Banjo as they talked about where this scruffy cat could have come from. Lauren seemed to love him instantly and Banjo was certainly enjoying all the attention. LuLu and Boo immediately felt better seeing how delighted everyone appeared with this stranger who had snuck in the house.

Soon after, Lauren decided it was time for her to leave but said she couldn't go without this lovable cat. Lauren wanted to take Banjo with her, give him a bath, and perhaps a new home. Banjo seemed very happy with this idea as he had not left her lap since she arrived, and it was clear he loved her back.

LuLu and Boo were happy, too. Earlier that day they were sure this smelly and messy cat was going to upset their owners, but just the opposite happened. Banjo brought happiness and love with him along with his crazy and wild behaviour. Lauren, Sam, and Quinn loved and accepted him just the way he was. They were all enjoying their time together when, to LuLu's great delight, a can of delicious salmon loaf was opened and put out for three cats to share.

About the Author

Roxanne Rudkin is a Canadian author and registered nurse. She lives with her husband and two cats, Daisy and Finnigan. This is her second book in the adventures of LuLu and Boo.